MAGIC THINGS

A CHAPBOOK

D1361919

MAGIC THINGS

MAGIC THINGS

A CHAPBOOK

by

Gregory Miller

**Illustrations by
John Randall York**

West Arcadia Press

Magic Things: A Chapbook
Copyright © 2022 Gregory Miller

ISBN-13: 9798417376887

West Arcadia Press
gmillerwriter@gmail.com

First printing: February 2022

Cover and interior art by John Randall York
Cover layout by Alexis George
Layout, formatting, and design by Anne Hardin

Other Books by Gregory Miller

"The Uncanny Chronicles"

The Uncanny Valley
Tales from a Lost Town

Darkness in the Valley
An Uncanny Dossier

Short Story Collections

Scaring the Crows
21 Tales for Noon or Midnight

On the Edge of Twilight
22 Tales to Follow You Home

Crows at Twilight
An Omnibus of Tales

Dark Nights and Candlelight
31 Tiny October Tales

For Alexis, with love

Table of Contents

Magic Things

9

Applause

27

Postscript:

Applauding the Magic

63

"Real isn't how you are made …
It's a thing that happens to you."

Margery Williams Bianco,
The Velveteen Rabbit

Magic Things

"Well, it's quite a sight," said Mr. Bulger, standing back to take in the three laden, glass-fronted bookcases in the old woman's otherwise humble study. "The finest collection of children's picture book first editions I've seen in ... thirty years? Forty? Hell, maybe ever."

"Thank you," said Mrs. Peggotty, allowing the shadow of a smile to cross her thin, care-worn face. "Forty years is about how long I've been collecting, give or take a few. I've kind of lost track. Sometimes it feels like I started just yesterday."

"Time does fly."

"No, it *runs*," Mrs. Peggotty corrected him. "Runs fast, runs forward, runs away, runs out."

Mr. Bulger steepled his fingers beneath his craggy nose. There was no need for a dramatic lead-up to the value. He was the professional appraiser, but Mrs. Peggotty knew very well what she had.

And it was nothing short of extraordinary.

There, on the top shelf of one case, was a row of Dr. Seuss hardcovers, all with dust jackets, all first state, including a *Cat in the Hat* with every necessary issue point: single signature binding, 200/200 price on the front flap, "For Beginning Readers" printed in black against blue on the cover. That alone was worth four thousand, possibly quite a bit more if the planets aligned. One shelf down, a pristine first of Burton's *Mike Mulligan and his Steam Shovel* rubbed bindings (through protective glassine wraps, of course) with Leaf's *The Story of Ferdinand*, which, in turn, leaned against an original 1942 printing of the Reys's *Cecily G. and the 9 Monkeys*. Beneath *that*, a notable copy of Silverstein's *The Giving Tree*, signed and dated by the author in the year of publication, stood at attention in a sharp, original dust jacket – miraculously untorn by small hands and unfaded by time.

And Mrs. Peggotty had *twelve shelves* of such treasures.

"*Madeline* is still my favorite," she said. "Well, that and *The Little House*. And *Little Toot*. And … Oh, goodness, I love them all."

Tears glassed the retired librarian's eyes.

Mr. Bulger cleared his throat, pretending not to notice. "Well, Mrs. Peggotty, if you want a conservative estimate, I'd say $450,000 for the lot. With a bit of luck and on a good day, you're looking at half a million."

"Yes." Mrs. Peggotty nodded, voice calm. "That's what I figured."

"If you wanted to sell …"

"Thank you, Mr. Bulger, but no. I know what your cut would be, and I need every cent. In three weeks, my niece is taking them down to the auction house in New York. Even with their commission, I'm certain the books will make more there than you can offer."

He sighed. "Undoubtedly." Then he smiled. "Maybe I'll bid on a few myself."

"I'd like that. And goodness, that would be fitting. We go way back, don't we, Mr. Bulger? How many years have you been my rare book bloodhound? Twenty-five?"

"At least. I hate to see your collection dispersed, Mrs. Peggotty. It's a work of art in and of itself."

Mrs. Peggotty limped slowly over to her rocking chair and eased herself down. "It's for a good cause. My husband was killed at Normandy, Mr. Bulger. I never remarried, never had children. But I worked as a librarian for fifty-five years, and that's where I found my family ... so *many* books, and so many little boys and girls to read them. The stories in books give across the years and generations. When you open a book, the author speaks, the illustrator inspires, out comes love, and that love is returned, making the pages breathe. It's the only kind of immortality that's real, and certainly the only kind that matters. I curated that love for over half a century. What a gift."

"But do you open *your* books, locked behind glass so much of the time?"

She nodded. "Sometimes. They're old friends. I love the paper, the art, the type, the *history* of first editions — touched by the first children to ever read them when those stories were new. But now they'll survive elsewhere, and serve a better purpose. The Still Creek Public Library will be spared, too."

"I wish you luck with the sale, then. And truly, it's been my pleasure." Mr. Bulger knew without being told that Mrs. Peggotty would only give up her collection if she also anticipated giving up far more than that before long.

"It's been larks, Mr. Bulger. Larks from start to finish. If you could send the formal, itemized appraisal soon, I'll forward it to the auction house when my niece delivers the books."

After Mr. Bulger departed, Mrs. Peggotty sighed, then, experiencing a now all-too-familiar wave of dizziness, took herself slowly off to bed. Once situated beneath her cool sheets and warm quilt, she thought vaguely, *I should have said more. I should have told him that books aren't just immortality … they're* magic. *But surely he knows that already. Gracious! If he didn't, how empty all those books would seem!*

She looked around the darkened room, then toward the gloom of the study. Ghosted by early moonlight, the glass of the bookcase doors shimmered with the bellows of her breath.

"Goodnight, Moon," she murmured.

Moments later the moonlight steadied, the shimmering ceased.

A major auction house in the hours leading up to an important sale is a frenetic place filled with frenetic people, however cultured, yet Mr. Bulger, unruffled, moved through the bustling throng with quiet, steady purpose. He was looking for someone, and soon found her in a far corner of the gallery: a smartly-dressed, severe-faced woman firmly entrenched in life's middle years, well-preserved but brittle, talking earnestly with the event coordinator ... a schmoozer named Claude Fellows, with whom Mr. Bulger had dealt before. Tens of thousands of wonders passed through Mr. Fellowes's galleries, yet none ever seemed to move him. But the business of it ... *that* made his face gleam with cool, eager sweat, his hands rub together in anticipatory earnestness.

Mr. Bulger didn't interrupt, just came over and stood so close to the woman, staring at her so pointedly, that her conversation with Mr. Fellows faltered, then ground to an awkward halt.

Finally she turned, looked him up and down, and iced a false smile. "Can I help you?"

"Miss Flint?" he inquired, though he knew she was; he'd seen a framed photo of her in Mrs. Peggotty's study.

Her nod was minute, almost imperceptible.

"Bertram Bulger, rare book dealer and the appraiser of your aunt's collection." He kept both hands clasped behind his back. "I'm ... sorry for your loss."

She stared at him a moment, and her face — already mildly austere, faintly humorless, perceptibly aloof — took on a cooler tinge. Even the façade-smile faltered.

"Ah, Mr. Bulger!" said Mr. Fellows, "Come to check the accuracy of your —"

"If I could have three minutes of your time," Mr. Bulger said to Miss Flint, ignoring Mr. Fellows entirely.

"So glad you could come, Mr. Bugler —"

"Bulger."

"*Bulger*," corrected Miss Flint. "But as you can imagine, things are a bit hectic just now. The auction begins in moments, and several reserve prices are —"

"The auction doesn't begin for another *forty-five minutes*. I only need three."

Miss Flint sighed, cast a look at Mr. Fellows, nodded, and waited while he stepped away with a churlish sniff.

"Good turnout," Mr. Bulger noted.

Miss Flint said nothing, eyeing him with cautious distaste.

"Interesting thing," Mr. Bulger continued. "I sent a copy of the collection's estimate to the Still Creek Public Library last month, and received some *very* sad and shocking news in reply. You undoubtedly know that, because I left several messages for you about it and also sent a certified letter, which you signed for."

Miss Flint's teeth gleamed through slightly parted lips.

"It's been a hectic few months," she replied. "Time flies following the death of a loved one, especially during the oversight of an estate."

"And an auction," added Mr. Bulger. "'Hectic.' Yes, you've used that word twice now. Everything is all so *hectic*, you say. Lord Byron wrote, 'The busy have no time for tears.'"

"Who?"

"Never mind."

"I have no time to be quoted at," said Miss Flint, "and I'm not at all certain I care for your insinuation."

"Nor should you be, because offense was most decidedly intended."

She pursed her lips, eyes frost and fire, then turned away.

"Why?" Mr. Bulger asked, directing the question at her back. "Your aunt's legacy – the only legacy she cared about – is in your hands, and you're throwing it away by keeping the money for yourself."

"If it meant so much to her, she should have modified her will. A handshake agreement doesn't cut it in court."

He pressed on. "The library will close, you know, and the next-closest to Still Creek and half a dozen other towns is over fifty miles away. Why?" he repeated. "Why do this?"

Miss Flint turned back to face him. "Her legacy … it wasn't about me. *Never* was. My aunt was a selfish person, Mr. Bugler."

"Bulger."

"Selfish and misguided."

"She told me everything else in her estate would go to you. That, and twenty percent of the proceeds from the auction."

"Ha!" The laugh was venomous. "And eighty percent to strangers."

Mr. Bulger sighed. "They weren't strangers to Mrs. Peggotty. The children, the librarians, the books, the authors. No, to her they were family, Miss Flint. And that library was home."

"And what was *I*, then?" she demanded, her voice shrilling just enough to turn some nearby heads.

"Someone she loved enough to always speak of fondly, and trusted enough to rely on when it came to the matters she cared about most."

Miss Flint took a step closer, now fully re-engaged. "I'm pragmatic, Mr. Bugler. You're a businessman. You must have some of that, too. My aunt, though? She was an escapist. Always running away into fantasy, into books, into her own head. And look where she ended up! Old and alone in a decrepit, dry-rotted bungalow, sitting on a fortune of moldy paper than never did her any good, with plans to leave that fortune to an institution that time and technology will eventually close down anyway as the world moves on."

"You say 'escapist' like it's a bad word," Mr. Bulger began, his mettle raised … then stopped. Fatigue washed over him like a heavy gray blanket. Mrs. Peggotty's niece was now a disappointment twice over. Not only had she flagrantly ignored her aunt's last wishes, but her reasons for doing so were so ... so ... What was the word?

Tedious.

Greed and ignorance. A mind-numbing combination so banal, so common, so *empty*, boredom threatened to match his outrage.

With great effort he managed to restrain both.

Mr. Bulger wouldn't explain the beauty of libraries to her – the feel of them, the smell of them. Nor their importance – to communities, to individuals, to body and soul ...

The hell with it. No point.

"Do you know why I sell books, Miss Flint?" he asked simply.

But Miss Flint had evidently had enough. "If you'll excuse me, Mr. Bugler, I really –"

Suddenly, shockingly, interrupting the last rites of the dying conversation, a breathless and heated Mr. Fellows ran up, three other house experts close on his coattails. They were all holding books. One, Mr. Bulger noted, was the pristine copy of *Mike Mulligan* he had personally acquired for Mrs. Peggotty over twenty years before. It had taken him half a decade to find one in such fine condition.

"Miss Flint? Could we have a word, please? I … You need to see …"

They huddled together.

They opened the books.

They flipped the pages.

Miss Flint saw.

As the flurry of exclamations and incredulity, recriminations and outrage reached fever pitch, Mr. Bulger strode calmly away and did not look back. Behind him, Miss Flint shrieked, "*Every single page? HOW many others? No ... They can't all ... Find out, then! It's not possible! It's not ... There must be ... You can't possibly ... BLANK?*"

"I sell books," Mr. Bulger finished to himself, "because they're *magic*, Miss Flint.

"But," he added, voice laden with quiet sorrow, "I don't suppose you will ever understand."

"A book must be the axe
for the frozen sea within us."

Franz Kafka,
from a letter to Oskar Pollack

Applause

He came in through the oiled brass doors and walked across the smooth, shoe-worn tile so quietly, Eliza Gerts didn't even notice him until she chanced to pause from stamping books and glance up. When she did, there he was, standing silently on the other side of the counter not four feet away. She yelped, then clapped a hand to her mouth, although the library was otherwise empty.

He was young, probably a third her age … eighteen, nineteen, she guessed. Too thin. Neat but faded, slightly threadbare clothes. Anemic complexion. And his eyes …

Eliza couldn't see his eyes. He kept them firmly fixed on the floor, a shock of unkempt brown hair veiling them.

"Can I help you?" she asked softly, perfunctorily.

He shifted from one foot to the other but said nothing.

"Sir?"

At this his lips moved, something whispered out, but Eliza just shook her head. For perhaps the first time in her long career as a librarian, she said, "I'm sorry, sir, can you speak up a bit?"

The noise, faint as lazy wind through green leaves, now resolved itself into words: "There's no need to call me 'sir,' ma'am."

She paused, then nodded slightly, waiting for the young man to follow up the statement with, "My name is ..." or, simply, "I'm ..."

He didn't.

"What *should* I call you, then?" She noticed her palms had broken out in a light sweat. He was beginning to make her uncomfortable. His eyes, still on the floor ... Eliza wondered if he was guilty of something; or, worse, if he was planning to do something that would make him feel guilty *after* ...

She darted a look at the phone on the counter, just inches from her hand, and at the red *Emergency* button in the lower right corner of its face.

"Charlie," he whispered.

"Charlie?" she repeated.

He nodded. And now Eliza noticed something else: he'd smiled when she said his name. It was just a flicker, a twitch, but a smile nonetheless. A good one, too; nothing fake or cynical about it. Slowly, almost imperceptibly, her palms began to dry.

"Charlie, do you want to register for a library card? I don't think I've seen you in here before."

He shook his head. "I don't like to read," he murmured.

Eliza blinked.

"I need a job," he added, wincing as if expecting her to lash out and strike him. When no blow fell, he continued in the same thin voice, "There's a sign in the window. You need a night caretaker. I can clean and look after things real fine. I'm good at it."

Eliza could have kicked herself. The *sign*. Up for so long, unanswered and ignored, it had become a meaningless fixture. Careless, careless.

"Oh, Charlie, I'm sorry. That sign was put up before the board cut our funding. I should have taken it down months ago. Right now the library can't afford …" Then she stopped, because at that moment, for the first time, Charlie raised his head and swept the hair from his face. The irises of his eyes were a deep brown, but the sclerae were red and his cheeks damp.

"Please, ma'am," he said, desperation creeping into his voice, though it still hadn't risen above a whisper. "I haven't eaten in a while. I'll do a real fine job and won't cause trouble. I'll work cheap."

"How long since you ate, Charlie?"

He thought a moment. "I had two granola bars and some string cheese yesterday afternoon."

Eliza thought a long moment – of the library's reduced budget, but also of the young man standing before her … his wind-tunnel voice, strange mannerisms, but most of all his smile – faint, fleeting, but *honest*.

She sighed. "All right then, Charlie, come on around and take a seat. Let's see if there's any numbers we can crunch. But first, soup and sandwiches. As much and as many as you want."

Margie Wilks, the young assistant librarian, smiled ruefully. "Well, you did fine by hiring him, Miss Gerts. He'll work hard and do as he's told. But he's a wounded dog. Not the kind that takes a beating then goes all mean. The kind that slinks off under the porch and dies. Timid as a mouse and shyer than a shadow. Don't expect much in terms of personality."

"You *know* him?" Eliza locked the library doors with a big iron key, and together they walked down the steps into the gathering summer dusk.

"Oh, sure. Most do, I would think. Or know him to *see* him, at least. He's a couple years older than me, and lived here his whole life."

"He doesn't look a day over nineteen!"

"He's twenty-six."

Eliza stopped walking. "You're *kidding*. How's that possible? I don't believe it."

"He lived near me for as long as I can remember," said Margie. "The driveway to the Halloway farm is out past the end of Grant Street. Back in the day we rode the bus together, had a few classes together, talked a bit now and then ... I know him. And he's twenty-six. Cross my heart."

"*Halloway*. Any relation to George, who passed ... when ... back in April?"

Margie nodded. "Charlie's father. And a meaner old cuss you'd never want to meet."

"Oh, I met him all right, and you're not wrong. Tried to block every grant we ever got, and now and then he'd send us letters about some book he wanted banned or some program he wanted cancelled. Lord, the grammar in those letters was enough to make a body's skin crawl, let alone the language."

They walked on in silence for a time. Then Margie said, "When a child is put down by his old man every day of his life, and beaten every night his old man comes back from a bender — and there were *lots* of those — that child will either turn out just like his old man, or just like Charlie: harmless but haunted. Last month they foreclosed on the farm ... Mr. Halloway left too many debts. That's the only thing that'd drive a man like Charlie out into town, let alone to work in a public place. Desperation. He has to eat."

"A pigeon among the cats," Eliza replied. "He looks young because he's terrified." The streetlamps blinked on. Their shoes clicked on the cobbled street as they passed the cigar store, the barbershop, the druggist, and reached the darker residential blocks.

They stopped by Eliza's front walk. "Where's he living *now*, then?" she asked.

"From what I hear, the motel on Joiner Street. He's been doing odd jobs all over town these last few weeks. I tried talking to him a couple of times. He's kind, Miss Gerts. Smart, too. Thoughtful, though all that may be buried now. He wouldn't speak to me, though. Probably embarrassed. Embarrassed and scared."

"That's awfully sad."

Margie shrugged. "Who knows? It's unlikely, but maybe that'll change. He has a dependable job now, thanks to you. Goodnight, Miss Gerts. See you in the morning."

Eliza opened the unlocked door and let herself in. Home … the only truly warm and safe place to be. And she thought of Charlie out there, alone in a tatty motel room on Joiner Street.

"Goodnight."

"Locking up for the night now, Miss Gerts."

Two weeks had passed, and Charlie, working from eight in the evening to seven in the morning, toiled with a systematic thoroughness and dedication none could fault. The library was immaculate: oaken desks and brass lamps polished, high shelves dusted, slate floor tiles scrubbed. But despite the good work and Eliza and Margie's praise, he still never spoke until spoken to unless it was about work – nor looked anyone in the eye unless absolutely necessary.

Eliza waved him over.

He wheeled the bucket and mop to the front desk. She noticed his new work shirt and trousers were freshly pressed and spotless, as they always were at the start of his shift. *Washes and irons them every day*, she thought. She had given him a two weeks' advance on his wages, and Margie had informed her that he was now renting a room from O'Connor's Boarding House two blocks away – certainly an improvement over the motel on Joiner. Fresh clothes and a decent place to stay. It was a start – humble but undeniable.

"Yes, Miss Gerts?"

"Charlie, tell me something."

He waited silently for the question, eyes glued to the soapy water in his bucket. Confronted with that silence, Eliza chose her words with care.

She wanted to ask many things: *Do you have any friends? What do you think about? What do you fear? Do you dream? What do you* do *all day besides sleep and work? What do you* enjoy *doing?*

And, most of all, *What can I do?*

Instead she said, simply, "Charlie, why don't you like to read?"

He cleared his throat. He shifted from one foot to the other and back again. He ran a hand through his hair.

Eliza went on quickly, "I don't want to make you uncomfortable. It's just that I've made a career of curating books, and I'm always curious why some people enjoy them and others don't."

Still nothing. Just that shifting from one foot to another, that hand through the hair, a pulse beating fast and hard in his temple.

Suddenly it occurred to her. "Charlie … *can* you read?"

The response was immediate. "Oh yes, Miss Gerts! I can read. I didn't do great in school, but I can read."

"Then why don't you like it?"

He swallowed. "Daddy made me read the Bible to him every night. Because *he* couldn't, you see. Twenty pages a night, and the print was real small. Made my throat hurt and my head ache. And I didn't much care for it, except for the Sermon on the Mount, but he almost always had me read *Revelation*."

Eliza nodded. "Any other books in your house, Charlie?"

"Some *bad* books." He whispered the word "bad" even more quietly than the rest. "I saw them in Daddy's closet."

"Oh. *Oh*." She paused. "Any others?"

He shook his head. "Daddy frowned on others. I read some of the books we covered in school, but it wasn't easy since he didn't like them in the house. There was *Of Mice and Men*, *Lord of the Flies*, *Hamlet*. A handful more. But I can't say I enjoyed them, having to keep the reading to a schedule and hide them at home."

She shook her head, knowing he wouldn't see it. "Well, thank you, Charlie. I'm sorry to have bothered you about it."

"No bother, Miss Gerts."

He turned to go.

"Charlie, could I ask just one more thing?"

He slowly turned back, slowly nodded.

"When you're alone among the bookshelves every night, what do you hear?"

He cleared his throat, and she wondered if despite his shyness, his total lack of self-esteem, he was silently questioning her sanity. "Nothing, Miss Gerts. Just me. Everything else is quiet and still."

When he was gone, the squeak of the bucket wheels faint in some distant aisle, Eliza leaned back in her chair, fingers tented below her nose, and thought, thought, and thought some more.

৩৯

"Miss Gerts?"

"Hmm?"

It was early morning, the library was about to open, and Charlie was about to sign off. He stood before her, all nerves and jitters, holding a book under his arm.

"Found this out on a table, Miss Gerts. I know you and Miss Wilkinson shelve 'em, so I set it aside. I guess you missed it before you went home."

"Oh! Margie and I must have been in a rush. We're usually not that careless. Thank you, Charlie."

"Um … Miss Gerts, the only thing is, the book was still open to a certain page, and the page was vandalized. I knew you'd want to know, so I brought it to show you."

"Gracious! Let me see."

He handed it over.

"Well, it's hardly vandalism, thank goodness. Someone found a poem and penciled a star by it. Must be a favorite. Not the best thing to do to a public book, but far from the worst."

"Oh, that's good."

Eliza smiled, gazing at the page. "It's a good poem, too. Did you read it, by chance? I always enjoy reading what others before me felt worthy of noting."

"No, ma'am."

"Want a look now?"

"Ah. Um. I guess."

She handed the book back to Charlie and watched him read, noting the slow, measured time he devoted to each short line. And when he reached the last quatrain, she mouthed the words in time to the movement of his eyes:

> *It matters not how strait the gate,*
> *How charged with punishments the scroll,*
> *I am the master of my fate:*
> *I am the captain of my soul.*

Charlie looked up. "That was pretty good. And you're right, it's nice to see someone liked it. Even so, I'm not sure I understand it."

"That's OK. Reading can surprise you. Sometimes you'll be walking along, minding your own business, and a line from a poem or story will come to you, even if you read it years before. And all of a sudden it will make sense."

"What does it mean to you?"

"Well," she said, and noticed that for the first time since meeting Charlie, she hadn't needed to lean forward to hear him; he was *interested*, faintly but most definitely. "It can mean different things to different people, and that's just fine. But to me, I'd say William Henley is taking control with this poem. He's saying that all the grief and pain of life can't break him. And that not even death can, either. His soul is his own."

That brief, sincere smile surfaced, then went back into hiding beneath the tremulous mask of shyness. "That must be nice, to believe something like that," Charlie said, and handed back the book.

ഔൟ

"Do you really think you can change him?"

Margie and Eliza sipped their coffee. Laura's Diner buzzed like a hive around them, Laura herself bellowing orders like a queen bee somewhere in the back.

"Me? No. Not alone at least," said Eliza. "And 'change' is the wrong word. Strengthen? Restore? Fortify, maybe? But," she added, squinting at the faint cup ring on the table, "I do think I can nudge him in the right direction."

"He's a sweet man," said Margie. "A good man, too," she added, almost as an afterthought. "I hope you're right."

Eliza raised her eyebrows.

Margie added a packet of sugar to her coffee. "Back when we were kids, my dad used to love fixing old bikes for me and my brothers. In those days, when I looked at Charlie, talked with him on the bus, walked with him now and then, I'd think of him in those terms … I knew he was damaged, neglected — a beater no one would want, at least in *his* view. But I hoped maybe if someone offered to strip off and polish up all the years of rust and corrosion, hammer out the dents and dings, replace a part or two, throw down a new coat of paint and thread some streamers through the spokes, Charlie would let that happen. And after, he'd see himself all fixed up, know what to do ... *and do it.*"

"But now you doubt that's possible."

"Yes, I guess I do. Other people ... they've tried before and failed."

"You mean *you* tried and failed?" Eliza asked gently.

Margie shrugged. "I suppose that's neither here nor there."

"*All change is a miracle to contemplate; but it is a miracle which is taking place every instant.*"

"Thoreau."

Eliza nodded. "It gives me hope."

"You know Thoreau burned down a whole damn forest that belonged to Emerson, don't you? And that his mother's house was in walking distance of Walden Pond? He wasn't the sage of the wilderness most people think."

"Well, I'm sure the former was an unfortunate accident and the latter a shrewd choice. It's easier to appreciate nature with Mom's home cooking right down the road."

Margie clinked her empty cup down on the table. "See? You give people the benefit of the doubt no matter what ... You don't even *need* that quote."

"You're right. But having it doesn't hurt."

ॐ

"Another book, Miss Gerts!" said Charlie the next morning. "And it's marked just like before."

"Oh? Which is it this time?"

He handed it over. Eliza glanced at the noted lines.

"Dickinson!" she exclaimed. An old man sitting at a nearby table stopped reading the *Still Creek Gazette* long enough to scowl at her. She apologized softly.

"Dickinson," she repeated in a whisper. "Did you read it?"

"Yes ma'am, this time I did. I liked it." Gently, he took the book back and recited,

> *To see the Summer Sky*
> *Is Poetry, though never in a book it lie —*
> *True Poems flee.*

"Do you like walking outside in the summertime?" she asked Charlie.

"No, ma'am," he said, taking off his name tag.

"Why not? Too hot?"

"No. Too many people. I like to be … I'm more comfortable alone."

Eliza nodded, sighing.

"Miss Gerts?"

She looked up, surprised to find Charlie meeting her gaze without prompting.

"I heard something last night, Miss Gerts. It was … Oh, maybe I shouldn't say."

"No, please! I'd like to know."

"It was … well, like a whisper, I guess."

"A whisper?"

Charlie nodded.

"What kind of a whisper?"

"I don't know for sure, Miss Gerts. But then that bit of poetry by Mr. Henley came to mind.

Just like you said it would. And some of it made sense, and got me to thinking. And then I saw *this* poem. And maybe …" He paused, took a deep breath, and continued, "Maybe I'll take a little walk in the park today after all. That's what Miss Dickinson is suggesting, isn't it?"

"I'd say so, yes. And it certainly is a beautiful day for a stroll."

"Maybe so. Yes, maybe it is."

"And Charlie?"

He turned back.

"Be sure to look up at the sky, too."

He left, smiling faintly.

Captain of my soul, Eliza thought, and went back to stamping books.

Another book found that night, another talk the next morning. "And *two* whispers now," Charlie said excitedly. And they spoke of the new quote he'd found:

> *In the depth of winter, I finally learned that within me there lay an invincible summer.*

"Albert Camus," Eliza said, nodding. "Take it home with you."

"I need a library card, ma'am," Charlie said.

That night he heard *three* whispers, and found a fourth book left out on one of the tables, open, yet another quote marked with a little star.

❧

In the days and weeks that followed, Eliza plied Charlie with passages about loss and love, strength and vulnerability, grief and joy, fortitude and friendship. About nature and seasons, youth and age, life and death. She fed him Wordsworth and Coleridge, Shelley and Auden, Melville and Hemingway, Bradbury and Steinbeck, Frost and Fitzgerald. Some resonated with him, others didn't. Some struck him instantly, others took time. Yet as July gave way to August and August to September, she increasingly found herself smiling in silent approval at the gradual changes taking place in the young man.

"He walks the streets now," Margie said over an early-autumn supper at *Cookin' Cousins Cuisine*. "He nods at the men and tips his hat at the ladies!"

"The ladies? Or just you?"

Margie blushed. "Eliza, the *idea*."

"I've seen you talking with him, Margie. No, no, I wasn't peeping. But on my walks I've seen you approach him more than once. He's still shy, but the smile that lights up his face after your words with him should be captured in a painting."

"Well, it makes me happy. I thin ..." She trailed off. "Anyway, I even saw him waving at a couple of kids. And Francine Morrison claims he tried out for the Still Creek Hornets!"

"Baseball," Eliza said. "He recently read some portions of *The Natural.*"

"Full of good quotes on the game, that's for sure."

"Yes," said Eliza, "but more than that." And she recited, "*We have two lives, Roy, the life we learn with and the life we live with after that. Suffering is what brings us toward happiness.*"

"Wonderful."

"By the way, you know what he told me yesterday?"

Margie raised her eyebrows.

"He said the library *hums* for him now. Voice after voice, murmuring from the darkened shelves."

"Good heavens! What does *that* mean?"

Eliza stared at Margie for a long time, appraising her, truly looking at her young friend, plumbing the depths behind her deep green eyes.

"I hear them too, Margie. Every day, from the time I walk into this building and all through the hours until I leave. Don't you?"

Now it was Margie's turn to stare at *her* friend, mind working, thoughts racing, until suddenly, as if a switch had flipped, her eyes lit up.

"Yes, Eliza," she said, voice firm. "Oh, yes. Yes indeed, I do."

ৡৣৡ

Another month passed. October swept in on a cold wind that spoke through dried leaves and rustling corn stalks. All through town people heard it. And, hearing, they picked out pumpkins, pressed and fermented late-season apples, lit wood fires, and chose or made costumes.

October was Eliza's favorite month. Every year she transformed the library basement into a haunted house, the aisles into catacombs, the books into bones interspersed with bottles of amontillado. Every Halloween night she turned herself into a witch, led the library games for wide-eyed children, then went to the Halloween dance. Every year she waited for it. Every year she gloried in it. And every bleak November 1st, the magic muted, she mourned.

Yet this year … this year another darkness, slight but serious, disturbed the comfortable shadows of imagination and depressed her.

It was Charlie who had brought it … Poor Charlie, who, after making such strides, after hearing *such voices*, had fallen back into dissolute, sullen silence – which, no coincidence, mirrored the silence now *upon* him.

One short day before Halloween, on the morning of October 30th, Eliza could stand it no more.

"How was your shift?" she asked, turning on the lobby lights. Outside, the cool, pre-dawn wind rattled brittle branches against the tall gothic windows.

"Quiet, Miss Gerts," he said softly, eyes once more downcast. "Very, very quiet."

"The voices still silent, then?"

He nodded, body sagging like a wilted flower.

"No more marked books?"

"Oh, yes. The books still appear."

"Well, what's today's quote?"

Charlie led Eliza back to a far reading table. He clicked on a green-shaded brass lamp, pulled a worn old volume toward him, squinted, and read,

I know not all that may be coming,
but be it what it will, I'll go to it laughing.

"Melville!" she exclaimed. "Oh, what a clear vision he had of the world." But Charlie just stood there, listless and dour, staring at the book without seeing.

Eliza sighed. "Charlie, forgive me, but you're *not yourself*. Haven't been in almost three weeks, truth be told. What is it? What's troubling you?"

No smile, no expression. An invisible dark veil had fallen over his face. He shook his head.

"Please. Maybe I can help."

As his silence continued, she felt despair creeping up her spine … A deep, cold sadness that only manifested when all her best efforts threatened to turn to dust.

"The dance," he said abruptly, softly, simply.

"Beg pardon?"

"The dance," Charlie said again. "There was a quote some weeks back, and that got me to thinking about the Halloween dance. And ever since, I can't weigh up any other bits of writing. Just that one."

Eliza thought hard, but came up empty. "What was it?"

Immediately Charlie recited:

Fear is a cloak which old men huddle
About their love, as if to keep it warm.

"Wordsworth," he added.

Eliza nodded. "But what does that have to do with the dance?"

"I ..." He stopped, took a deep breath, then tried again. "There's someone. A young lady. She's kind to me. I'm not used to that. And –"

"Say no more." Eliza patted him on the shoulder.

"And she's beautiful," Charlie finished in a rush.

"You want to ask her to the dance? Why, it's simple. You're a handsome young man. You just go on up to her and –"

"I can't."

"But really, you just –"

"No, Miss Gerts. I can't. I *can't*."

He said it with such authority, such finality, such rising anger that it stopped Eliza short.

"I'm sorry," she said, hastily turning away. "I shouldn't be so presumptuous. I'm going to go run the numbers."

And she noticed, as she walked off with brisk but dejected strides, that the shelves had now fallen silent for her, too. It was a deafening hush. An emptiness.

An absence.

ভ৵৶

The small back office smelled of old paper and cracked leather spines – the spice from a thousand far countries and years. To Eliza it was the smell of home.

"There now," said Margie. "You're a smart one. Clever, too. Even wise, now and then. But sometimes you miss the mark, if you'll forgive me saying so."

Eliza stopped dabbing her eyes and took a sip of tea.

"We *all* miss it now and then," Margie continued, softening the blow. "It happens. In this instance, what you missed is just how badly he's been hurt over the years. I told you back when you hired him … His father was the devil, Eliza, and that sweet man …"

Eliza was surprised to see Margie dab her own eyes too.

"No luck on your end either, then," she said gently.

"I knew it was probably a fool's errand, same as yours, but seeing him day in and day out rekindled old feelings. Even old hopes. We walked, we talked, we had coffee together, we shared good, quiet moments. And I caught glimpses, little glimmers like when we were kids. Behind that handsome face, underneath all that scar tissue, he's a beautiful soul. My God. And he's *so close.*"

Eliza nodded.

"But he has something he needs to do, and I can't do it for him," Margie continued. "I *won't.* He wants something, but desire isn't enough. You have to have the will to *see things through.* My grandmother told me bravery isn't the absence of fear … It's being scared to death, then doing what has to be done anyway. And that's a hurdle he hasn't cleared. Not yet, maybe not ever. And I can't *wait* forever. It breaks my heart, Eliza. Truly, it does."

Eliza leaned forward and took Margie's hand. "I know what he wants to do … The thing he wants to do but can't. I know what that is. I understand."

"Then you know just how much this hurts me as well as you."

"The library was working for him, Margie. He *heard the voices*. And now they're gone." She leaned heavily against her desk. "And, God help me, not just for him, either."

Margie rubbed her temples. "Remember, George Halloway didn't just use his fists, or a belt, or a hickory switch on Charlie. He used *words*, just as you did through books, just as I did through conversation. Words can tear down civilizations as well as build them up. Think what they can do to a sensitive person like him."

Eliza sniffed.

Margie continued, "He's lived his whole life thinking he's a burden to the world, all because of that wicked old cuss. That's a hard way to live, and a harder thing to cure in just a few short months, no matter how good the medicine. Our ministrations can give him a push in the right direction, but he can't thrive forever on words alone. At some point you – *we* – have to say, 'I've given him all the tools he needs. Now he has to build with them.' And at some point, he'll either do just that, or leave them rusting in the mud."

"And you think he'll let them rust."

"I'm not confident … but I suppose any degree of uncertainty leaves room for possibility." She reached into her purse, pulled out a slim volume, and flipped it open to a marked page. "This has helped me these last few days. It's not the same as leaving it on a table for you to find, but even so …" She handed it over.

Eliza looked at the spine. "Dickens," she said. "That dear, grand man." She looked at the page and read aloud, "*It's always something, to know you've done the most you could. But, don't leave off hoping, or it's of no use doing anything. Hope, hope to the last!*"

She brooded on this, then sipped her now-tepid tea. "How'd you get so canny?"

Margie allowed a small smile. "Osmosis, maybe. There's no better place in the world for it."

Halloween morning dawned on cascades of falling gold and russet leaves. Very early, pensive and nervy, Eliza unlocked the library's double doors and slipped quietly in. Usually she slept like a log, but she had been up much of the night. The previous evening, for the first time in weeks, she hadn't left a book out and open for Charlie to find. But now, after exhaustive hours spent in bedroom darkness, dim-lit study, more bedroom darkness, then the light of early dawn, she felt, through her exhaustion, that she had found the perfect quote. She would slip over, silent as a moth, leave it on a prominent reading table, and hope for the best. It was all she could think to do; the last card to play.

Once it was in place, open on the center table beneath a lit green banker's lamp where Charlie couldn't possibly miss it, she glided back to her spot behind the checkout desk and went about her morning duties. As she worked she could hear him, somewhere in the darkened aisles, as he finished his mopping – the soft tread of his shoes and the swish of the damp cotton strings on the worn and chipped tile.

Soon now, she thought, as Margie eased in backwards through the front door, two coffees in two hands, and handed one to her.

"How did you know?" Eliza said, touched and grateful.

"Because I didn't sleep either," she replied, and settled onto a stool to shuffle a new stack of card catalog entries and wait with breathless, poorly-concealed anticipation of her own.

Time is short, Eliza thought. *We* both *know it has to be now.*

They both looked up.

Charlie appeared from a back aisle. Without pausing, he walked quickly up the center of the long room between the tables. He'd *never* walked quickly before ... even during the weeks of his great discoveries, his gait had been slow, almost wary.

Now it was different.

"The book," Eliza murmured. "*See* it."

He didn't, striding past it without so much as a glance. Her heart fluttered and her hands went cold.

"Yes," whispered Margie. "Almost there."

Eliza looked at her, mouth slightly agape. "What?"

She shook her head. "Watch. And oh God, Eliza, *hope.*"

Charlie stepped up to the checkout counter. He turned to Eliza first ... and the first thing she noticed was that his eyes were bright, and maintained firm, resolute contact with hers.

"I'm sorry for yesterday, Miss Gerts," he said. "You were right. It really *is* simple. I just needed to work things through on my own. It took a while."

Eliza's chin quivered. "Are the voices back then, Charlie?"

He shook his head. "No. But they're waiting."

He turned to Margie. "Margie, forgive my forwardness, but you're a kind and pretty and … and *interesting* lady, and I like you very much. If you don't have plans, I'd be obliged to take you to the Halloween Dance tonight."

Without batting an eye or missing a beat, Margie replied, "Why, I'd be honored, Charlie Halloway."

He smiled. It lit up his face.

No, corrected Eliza, *it lit the whole room!* And she silently recited the quote by Victor Hugo she'd chosen … the quote Charlie had ignored, since he'd learned it already:

A library implies an act of faith.

Funny, he learned that faster than I ever did, she thought.

"There it is, Miss Gerts!" Charlie exclaimed, pointing over his shoulder. "Do you hear it?"

"My land," Eliza murmured, "I do at that."

The library fairly rang with it.

"Listen to those cheers!"

"And the *applause*," she added. "Why, Charlie, it's enough to bring down the house!"

It lasted so long he had to take *two* bows.

Postscript:

Applauding the Magic

I guess it was inevitable that I'd eventually write some stories about books and libraries. Any author who writes about those subjects is writing a love letter, because every author loves them. And we are drawn to write about what we love.

As it turns out, both of these stories percolated for a long time before I finally finished them. Here, for what it's worth, is a brief rundown of how they came about.

The idea for "Magic Things" took shape after I found a beautiful auction house catalog waiting for me in the mail ... I used to collect first editions by a handful of authors, so ended up on a lot of mailing lists for that sort of thing. The centerpiece of the auction was a collection of modern, classic children's book first editions. I flipped through the glossy, full-color pages of the catalog and was increasingly amazed – not only that some of the books had survived upward of a century in such fine condition, but also by the price estimates they commanded. There were scores of listings over dozens and dozens of pages, all with estimates in the thousands (if not tens of thousands) of dollars.

I knew straight away that whoever had built, maintained, and protected that collection – as it turns out, an elderly man who had recently passed away – had genuinely loved those books. Sometimes people collect things just for resale value or because it's the popular thing to do, but he had carefully, meticulously curated this gathering for over *forty-five years*. That's dedication, and dedication only comes from passion. The whole feel of it suggested genuine care.

Imagine immersing yourself in the history of childhood wonder for *decades*, learning everything there is to know about the books that helped to make us who we are and collecting the finest copies. Others could therefore still open them up and read them, however carefully, and in doing so connect with children from other times, other places – many of them old, old, old, or even long gone, but still, somehow, alive and young in the shared experience, safely tucked away in those carefully preserved pages, inks, and bindings. That is what a good collector does: gathers, protects, and appreciates, whatever the collection may be.

On the one hand I hated to think of those books at an auction house, their fates uncertain. On the other, I'm sure the old man had gathered many of those books at similar auctions. In such circumstances, one can only hope they all went to good homes, where their *true* worth, beyond estimates and insurance policies, is still being appreciated under a hundred different roofs ... and also that the original collector's intent for the collection had been honored.

But what about when such things are sold for the wrong reason? I took some notes on the idea, wrote a rough draft a few years later, then finally polished it up last fall, seven years after first receiving that catalog.

"Applause" had an even longer gestation, and I now know the exact date I came up with the idea: August 22, 2010, Ray Bradbury's 90th birthday. I was fortunate to have a close friendship with Ray, so was in Los Angeles to celebrate the occasion with him, his family, and a number of other friends. At the last minute, Ray didn't feel well enough to go out to the restaurant for the big party his family had planned, so we all brought the party back to him. And sometime during that afternoon, as we all talked and laughed throughout Ray's wonderful yellow house, Ray holding court from the big leather chair in his den, the idea zinged me. I know this because I jotted down some notes during the trip. The very last note for August 22nd reads, "Just began a new story, 'Applause,' after talking about it at Ray's party this afternoon." The very last note for the *following* day, the last full day of the trip, reads, "Ray again asked me to tell him about the new story I'm working on, 'Applause.' He loves the idea."

Until recently I had completely forgotten these details, to the point that I couldn't even pinpoint the year I'd started the story. I'm so glad my younger self had the foresight to take so many notes during those trips to see Ray. Time really does dull memory, like a current flowing constantly over a stone. And I'm so glad I uncovered that forgotten file now, today, on August 22, 2021, eleven years later to the very day, on what would have been Ray's 101st birthday.

Sometimes, when things come full circle (and they usually do, one way or another), they can take your breath away.

As for the idea – of a librarian using carefully-chosen quotes to inspire and heal – I have no doubt it was inspired by one of Ray's favorite anecdotes about how he wrote the first draft of what became *Fahrenheit 451* in the library of UCLA back in 1950. He typed like a madman on a rented typewriter in the basement, feeding it dimes to keep the timer going, then took breaks to run upstairs, crack open books, and gain inspiration from what he found within.

But what if someone works in a library, needs inspiration, but *doesn't read?* Someone who has potential, but lived with the cards stacked against him for so long that he can no longer see his own worth? A broken man? A lost soul?

In that case, it could be that someone *else* needs to prompt him – someone who sees that potential, and has an inkling, imperfect but promising, of how to unlock it. And who better to do that in a library than a librarian ... or two?

Books can be an immensely powerful tool when it comes to fortifying ourselves against the cruelties and difficulties of life; to stockpiling the strength and wisdom necessary to find our freedom, unfurl our wings, and take the great leaps of faith into the unknown that often mark the most important transitions we make.

That said, they cannot do the hard work for us – only mentor us, motivate us, then give us a gentle push in the right direction when their work is done. Ray once wrote, "… while our art cannot, as we wish it could, save us from wars, privation, envy, greed, old age, or death, it can revitalize us amidst it all." After that, the action is ours alone to take. Bolstered, we stand or fall based on our own resolve. As we should.

That is the great power of reading, and in "Applause," Charlie isn't its only receptor. Eliza and Margie, in trying to help him, both learn additional nuances of that power too. In the end, they also apply *their* new knowledge – the necessary combination of wisdom and will put to action.

A final thought.

Recently I spent a few days in Great Barrington, Massachusetts. There's a perfect used bookstore there – the kind rapidly being swallowed up by online sales and inflated rent. But somehow it has survived: three narrow rooms warrened and crannied by shelves, milk crates, and tables. It even has a cat, as all used bookstores should, who sits on the counter or wraps itself into sleep on an overstuffed chair. Its name is Ripley.

In a small alcove in the second room, a lady and her young daughter sat in two painted, pint-sized wooden chairs. In this time of Covid, both wore masks, and they matched: Mom sported Dr. Seuss's Thing 1, and her daughter Thing 2.

They were in the middle of reading a book when I passed them, headed for the shelves marked FANTASY AND HORROR just a few feet away. "*And now here is my secret, a very simple secret,*" Mom read. "*It is only with the heart that one can see rightly; what is essential is invisible to the eye.*"

Her daughter wanted to see the picture. She showed her, then said, "Ok, we have to go meet Daddy now ... We're late!"

"More," the little girl said.

"Tell you what," Mom said, closing the book. "How about we buy it? Then we can read it as many times as you want."

So she took *The Little Prince* up to the counter and bought it.

She understood the magic, both simple and profound. And as they walked out the door, every book on every shelf broke into thunderous applause.

Gregory Miller
August 22, 2021

About the Author

Gregory Miller was born in State College, Pennsylvania and grew up in Columbia, Maryland. The author of nine books, he is currently at work on the third volume of *The Uncanny Chronicles*. Miller resides in Pittsburgh, where he has taught high school English for twenty years. His website/blog is:

authorgregorymiller.wordpress.com.

About the Illustrator

John Randall York was born in Tyler, Texas, where his head and heart were filled with ghost stories, dreams, and priceless experiences. Influenced by Peter Spier, Edward Ardizzone, Jack Davis, Victor Ambrus, and Joseph Mugnaini, he draws and paints to share his dreams and visions. John lives in the historic Brick Street District in Tyler, Texas with his wife, Ruth, whom he met in high school French class. His website is: johnrandallyorkart.com.

Made in the USA
Monee, IL
19 March 2022